Millions of Americans remember Dick and Jane (and Sally and Spot too!). The little stories with their simple vocabulary words and warmly rendered illustrations were a hallmark of American education in the 1950s and 1960s.

But the first Dick and Jane stories actually appeared much earlier—in the Scott Foresman Elson Basic Reader Pre-Primer, copyright 1930. These books featured short, upbeat, and highly readable stories for children. The pages were filled with colorful characters and large, easy-to-read Century Schoolbook typeface. There were fun adventures around every corner of Dick and Jane's world.

Generations of American children learned to read with Dick and Jane, and many still cherish the memory of reading the simple stories on their own. Today, Pearson Scott Foresman remains committed to helping all children learn to read—and love to read. As part of Pearson Education, the world's largest educational publisher, Pearson Scott Foresman is honored to reissue these classic Dick and Jane stories, with Grosset & Dunlap, a division of Penguin Young Readers Group. Reading has always been at the heart of everything we do, and we sincerely hope that reading is an important part of your life too.

The World of

Dick and Jane

AND FRIENDS

Published in 2004 by Grosset & Dunlap,
a division of Penguin Young Readers Group, 345 Hudson Street, New York, New York 10014.
GROSSET & DUNLAP is a trademark of Penguin Group (USA) Inc.
Printed in the U.S.A.

ISBN 0-448-43646-9   10 9 8 7 6 5 4 3 2 1

CONTENTS

BASIC READERS

THE NEW

Guess Who

Dick

Look, Dick.
Look, look.

Oh, oh.

Look, Dick.

Oh, oh.
See Dick.
Oh, see Dick.

Sally

Look, Sally.

Look, look.

See Jane.

Oh, Jane.

See Sally.

See little Sally.

Little, little Sally.

Look, Jane.

See funny Sally.

Oh, oh, oh.

Funny little Sally.

Help, Help

Look, Dick.

See Spot.

Oh, see Spot.

Help, help.

Oh, Jane.

See Spot.

Oh, see Spot.

Come, Jane, come.

Help, help, help.

Look, Dick.

See Spot and Sally.

Come see Sally.

See funny little Sally.

Sally Sees Something

Come, Sally.

Come and look.

Come and see Sally.

Funny little Sally.

Dick, Dick.

Help, help.

I see something.

Help, help, help.

I see something.

Look, Sally.

I see something.

I see Baby Sally.

Little Baby Sally.

Look, look.

See funny Baby Sally.

Something Funny

Look, Dick.

Look, look.

I see something funny.

Come and see.

Come and see Spot.

Oh, Jane.

I see something funny.

Come, Jane, come.

See Spot and Baby Sally.

Come and help.

Look, Dick.

See Jane help Spot.

Oh, see something funny.

See little Spot.

Funny little Spot.

Jane and Puff

Oh, Jane.

I see something.

Look, Jane, look.

Look here.

Come, Puff.
Come here.
Jump, little Puff.
Jump, jump.

Look, Baby Sally.

Come here and look.

See Puff.

Puff can help.

Puff can help Jane.

See Puff Go

Come here, Dick.

Come and see Puff.

See Puff play.

See Puff jump.

Puff can jump and play.

Oh, Mother, Mother.

Come and look.

See Puff jump and play.

See little Puff play.

Look, Mother, look.

See Puff jump and play.

Oh, oh, oh.

See Puff jump down.

See Puff jump and go.

Jump down, funny Puff.

Jump down.

Jump down.

Go, go, go.

Tim and Sally Help

Sally said, "Look, Mother.
I can help.
See Baby Sally help.
See little Tim help.
See little Tim go.
Oh, see little Tim go."

Sally said, "Look, Tim.
Look down here.
I see cookies.
I see cookies down here.
Cookies, cookies, cookies."

Sally said, "Come, Mother.
We can go.
Look here, Mother.
Cookies, cookies, cookies.
Come, Mother, come.
We can go."

Go Away, Spot

Dick said, "Down, Spot.
I can not play.
Down, Spot, down.
Go away, little Spot.
Go away and play."

Sally said, "Oh, Spot.

We see you.

Tim and I see you.

And little Puff sees you.

We see you, funny Spot."

Dick said, "Oh, oh, oh.
Go away, Spot.
You can not help.
You can not play here."

Sally said, "Run away, Spot.
Run, run, run."

Puff, Tim, and Spot

Sally said, "See Puff go.
Puff can jump down.
Puff can run away.
See little Tim.
Tim can not jump down.
Tim can not run away."

Dick said, "Come, Spot.
You and I can play.
Look here, Spot.
Cookies, cookies.
Jump, Spot, jump."

Dick said, "See Spot.
Oh, see Spot jump."

Jane said, "Mother, Mother.
We see something funny.
Come here.
Come here.
Come and see Spot."

Find Dick

Jane said, "I see you.

I see you, Sally.

I can find you.

I can not find Dick.

Help me, Sally.

Come here.

Help me find Dick."

Jane said, "Oh, Father.
I can not find Dick.
And we can not play.
Help me, Father.
Help me find Dick."

Father said, "Look, Jane.
Look, look, look.
You can find Dick."

Sally said, "Oh, oh.
I see Dick now.
Father and I see Dick.
We see funny Dick.
Look, Jane, look.
You can find Dick now."

Who Can Help?

Dick said, "Mother, Mother.
Come here.
I want you.
Come and help me.
Oh, Jane.
Oh, Father.
Who can come?
Who can come and help me?"

Dick said, "Go away, Spot.
You can not help me.
Oh, my.
Oh, my.
I want Mother.
Mother can help me.
Run, Spot, run.
Run and find Mother."

Dick said, "Oh, Spot.
Now I can come in.
You can help me.
Little Spot can help.
You can help me come in."

See What I See

Dick said, "Look, Sally.

Look down here.

See what I see.

See my big cookie.

See me and my big cookie.

You can see Spot here.

Spot wants my big cookie."

"Oh, oh," said Sally.
"I see Tim and me.
And now I see Puff.
Puff is in here.
I see little Puff.
Puff and Tim and me."

Sally said, "Look, Jane.
Look down here.
You can see Jane in here."

Jane said, "Oh, oh, oh.
Who sees what I see?
It is something funny.
It is not Jane."

Little Boat

Sally said, "See my boat.
I want my little boat.
I want my little boat in here."

Jane said, "Dick can get it.
Dick is big.
Dick can go and get it."

"Not now," said Dick.
"I can not get it now."

Jane said, "Come, Sally.
Come and play.
Here is Tim."

"I want my boat," said Sally.
"Who can get it for me?
Is Father here?
Father can get it for me."

Sally said, "Oh, oh, oh.

Come here, Dick.

See what I see.

See my little blue boat now.

See who wants my boat.

My little blue boat.

See who wants it now."

What Can Dick Make?

Jane said, "Look, Sally.
See what I can make.
It is big and yellow.
It is for Puff."

Sally said, "Look, Mother.
I can make something for Tim.
Jane can make something for Puff.
What can Dick make?"

Dick said, "I can make something.
Come and see what it is."

"Is it blue?" said Sally.
"Is it yellow?
Is it red?"

Dick said, "Oh, my.
It is red and yellow and blue.
Come and see what it is."

Jane said, "Look, Sally.
Dick can make something pretty.
See what Dick can make."

"I see it," said Sally.
"It is pretty.
What is it?"

Jane said, "Oh, Sally.
It is **Dick**."

See It Go

Father said, "Look in here.
You can find something.
Something you want."

Dick said, "Look, Jane, look.
Red, yellow, and blue.
Yellow is for me.
Who wants red and blue?"

Jane said, "I want blue.
Red is for Sally."

Dick said, "Come, Sally.
Come and get something.
Red for you and blue for Jane."

Sally said, "Oh, Dick.
Pretty, pretty.
Make it big.
Make it big, big, big."

Jane said, "Run, Spot.
Run away, Puff.
See what I see.
Run, run, run."

"Now look," said Dick.
"See my boat.
See my boat go.
I can make it go away.
See it go.
Oh, see it go."

Who Can Work?

Dick said, "See me work.
I can help Father.
I can get something.
Something for Father."

Dick said, "Look, Father.
Jane plays and plays.
You and Mother work.
And I work.
Jane can not work.
Jane is a little baby."

Father said, "Oh, Dick.
Jane is not a baby."

Jane said, "See me now.

I can do something.

See me work.

I can help Mother.

See what I can do.

Sally is a baby.

Sally can not work."

Mother said, "Oh, my.
Sally is not here.
Who can find Sally?"

Sally said, "Look, Mother.
See me in my little house.
I can work.
And Spot and Puff can work.
We can make a house.
A funny little house."

Find My Ball

Sally said, "I want my ball.
My pretty yellow ball.
Who can find it for me?"

Jane said, "Here is a ball.
See this blue ball, Sally.
Do you want this ball?"

Sally said, "I want my ball.
My ball is yellow.
It is a big, pretty ball.
And it is in this house.
Help me find it."

"It is not here," said Dick.

Sally said, "Where is my ball?
It is in this house.
Where, oh, where is it?"

"It is not here," said Dick.
"Not down here, Sally."

Sally said, "Oh, Spot.
Do you see my ball?
Where is it, Spot?
Go and get it."

Sally said, "Oh, Jane.

Look up.

Look up.

See where my ball is.

Oh, oh, oh.

Dick looks down.

Little Spot looks up.

And Spot finds my ball.

My pretty yellow ball."

A Big Red Car

Dick said, "Away I go.
Away in my big red car.
See me go, Sally."

Sally said, "I want a car.
Make two cars, Dick.
A car for you.
And a car for me.
Make two cars."

Dick said, "Oh, Sally.
You can come in my car.
In my big red car."

"I want a car," said Sally.
"Make one for me, Dick.
A little one for me."

Dick said, "Look, Sally.
I can do something.
See what I can do.
I can make a big, big car.
Two can get in this car now."

Dick said, "Here, Sally.

This will look pretty in my car.

I will make it go up for you.

See it go up, up, up.

Now get in my car."

"Away we go," said Sally.

"Away, away in a big red car."

Who Will Jump?

Dick said, "Look, Sally.
Do you see this?
Come with me.
You will see something funny."

Sally said, "Oh, Dick.

I see what you want to do.

You want to make me jump.

Oh, oh.

You want to make me jump."

Dick said, "Not you, Sally.

I want to find Jane.

I want to make Jane jump."

Sally said, "I see Jane.
Jane is in the house.
Oh, oh.
I want to go in the house.
I want to see Jane jump."

"Come with me," said Dick.
"Come in the house with me.
You will see something fun.
You will see Jane jump."

Dick said, "Now look, Sally.
Now you will see Jane jump.
One . . . Two . . ."
"Three," said Sally.
"One, two, three.
See Dick jump."

I See You

Jane said, "Come with me, Sally.

Come to the house with me.

Dick will not look here.

Not in the house.

Dick will not find you here."

Dick said, "Oh, oh.

I see something blue.

I can guess where Jane is.

One, two, three for Jane.

I see you, Jane.

One, two, three for you.

Come with me, Puff.

We want to find Sally now.

Where, oh, where is Sally?"

Dick said, "Oh, oh.

I see something yellow.

I can guess where Sally is.

One, two, three for Sally.

I see Sally with Jane.

One, two, three for Sally.

Now, little Puff.

Do you want to come with me?

We will get Jane and Sally."

Jane said, "One, two, three.
One, two, three for me.
And one, two, three for Sally.
Sally is with me."

Dick said, "Oh, funny me.
This is something yellow.
It is not Sally.
And this is something blue.
It is not Jane."

Guess Who

Sally said, "See the cars.

See the cars go up, up, up.

One, two, three.

Three little yellow cars."

Father said, "Oh, Baby Sally.
You can not play here.
This is where we work.
Here is a ball.
Run and play with the ball."

Mother said, "Spot, Spot.
Go to the house.
You can not play here.
Come with me to the house."

Jane said, "Come here, Dick.

Oh, come here.

Guess what I see.

Guess what Spot can make."

Sally said, "Oh, pretty, pretty.

Spot can make something pretty.

I can do what Spot can do.

I can make something pretty."

Jane said, "Oh, Father.
I want to do it."

Father said, "Come, Dick.
You and Jane can do it.
And here is little Puff.
I will help Puff do it."

Dick said, "Look, Mother.
See what we can make.
Guess who this is."

"Guess who this is," said Jane.

"Guess who this is," said Sally.
"And see the two little ones.
Guess who.
Guess who."

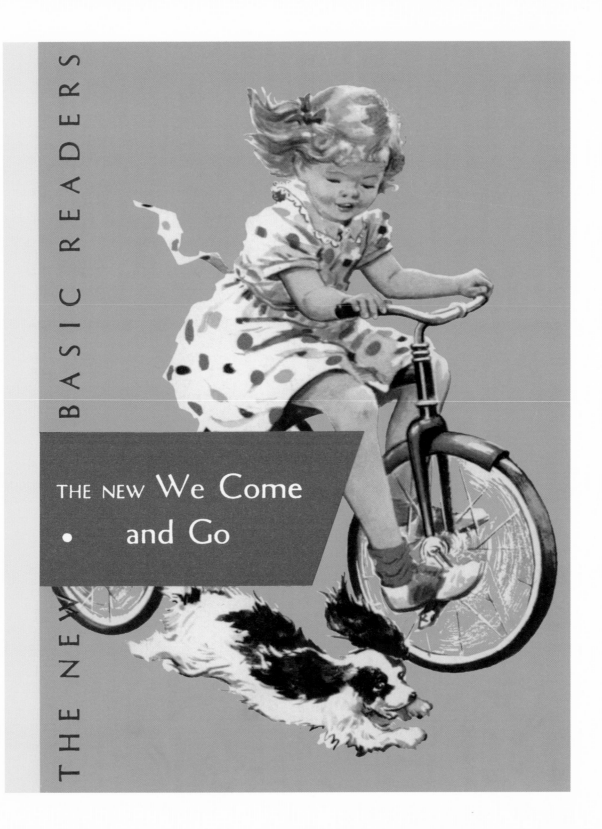

BASIC READERS

THE NEW We Come
• and Go

THE NEW

Come

Come, Sally.
Come, come.

Oh, Sally.

Come, come.

Come, Sally, come.

Oh, see.
See Sally go.

Go, Sally, go.
Go, go, go.

See Jane Go

Oh, Sally.
See Jane go down.
Down, down, down.
See Jane go down.

Look, Jane.
Look, look.
Oh, look.

Look, Tim, look.

Oh, look.

See funny, funny Jane.

See funny Jane go.

Sally and Mother

Sally said, "Oh, see.
See Mother go.
Come, Dick.
Come, Jane.
Come and go."

Jane said, "Oh, Dick.
See Sally and Tim.
Oh, oh, oh.
See Baby Sally go.
Go, Dick, go."

Sally said, "Oh, Mother.
See Dick go down.
See Jane go down.
Funny, funny Dick and Jane."

Tim and Baby Sally

Sally said, "Oh, Tim.
I see something.
Mother sees something.
Dick and Jane see something."

"Oh, oh," said Sally.
"I see something.
Something for Baby Sally.
And something for little Tim."

Sally said, "I see something.
Something for Dick and Jane.
And something for Sally.
I want something for Tim."

"Oh, look," said Dick.
"See something for little Tim."

Spot and Puff

Baby Sally said, "Look here.
I see something funny.
I see Spot and little Puff.
Spot wants something.
Puff wants something."

Jane said, "Look, Mother.
See Spot and Puff.
Spot and Puff want something."

Mother said, "Run, Jane.
Run, Dick.
Run and help little Sally.
Sally wants help."

"Oh, oh," said Baby Sally.
"Oh.

Oh.

Oh."

Little Tim Can Help

Dick said, "Look, look.
Here we come.
We can help."

Jane said, "Run, Dick.
Run, run.
We can help."

"Look, here," said Sally.

"One is for Dick.

One is for Jane.

And one is for Baby Sally."

"Look, Mother," said Sally.

"Here we come.

See little Tim.

Tim can help.

Tim can help Mother.

Oh, oh.

Tim is funny."

I See Three

"Here, Dick," said Mother.
"Here is something."

"I see three," said Dick.
"We want three.
I want a big one.
Jane wants a big one.
Sally wants a little one."

"One, two, three," said Jane.
"A big one for Dick.
A big one for Jane.
A little one for Baby Sally.
One, two, three."

"Oh, oh," said Sally.
"One, two, three.
One, two, three."

"See, see," said Father.
"One, two, three.
I see something funny."

"Run, run," said Sally.
"Here we come."

Father said, "Oh, oh.
Here I go."

Jump and Play

Sally said, "Oh, look.
Mother can jump.
Mother can jump and play."

Dick said, "Jump, Father.
You can jump.
You can jump and play."

"Look, Mother," said Sally.
"See Father jump.
See Father jump and play.
Big, big Father is funny."

Jane said, "Oh, Father.
You can not jump and play.
Spot can not jump and play."

Dick said, "Oh, see Puff.
Puff can jump.
Puff can jump and play."

We Make Something

"Look here," said Dick.
"I can make something funny.
I can make Spot.
Spot is red and blue."

"Oh, Dick," said Jane.
"I want to make something.
I want to make something blue."

"Look, Sally," said Jane.
"See my funny blue Puff.
Make something, Sally.
Make something blue."

"Oh, Jane," said Sally.
"I can not make Puff.
I can not make Spot.
I want to make little Tim."

"See me work," said Sally.
"I can make something blue.
See my funny blue Tim."

"Look, Sally," said Jane.
"Here is something for Tim.
Here is a funny red mother.
And a funny blue father.
A father and mother for Tim."

Play Ball

"Come, Jane," said Father.
"Come and play ball.
Come and play."

"Oh," said Jane.
"See the red ball go.
See it go up, up, up.
Run, Dick, run."

"Oh, oh," said Dick.
"Where is my ball?
I can not find it.
Come here, Jane.
Run and help me.
Help me find my red ball."

"I can help you," said Jane.
"We can find the red ball."

Dick said, "I see it.
I see the red ball.
Look, Father.
See where it is.
Come and help me."

Jane said, "Oh, Dick.
Spot can help you.
Spot can find the red ball."

Spot Finds Something

Dick said, "Come and work.

Come and help me.

I can not find the two boats.

I can not find my red ball.

Where is my yellow boat?

Where is the blue boat?

Where is my little red ball?

Where, oh, where?"

Jane said, "I can work.

I can find two boats.

Here is the yellow boat.

Here is the blue boat."

Sally said, "I can find cars.

See my little yellow car.

See my red car and my blue car.

Where is the red ball?

Where is my little Tim?"

Dick said, "Spot can work.
Spot can find the red ball.
Spot can help me."

Sally said, "See Spot work.
Spot can find Tim.
Spot can help me."

Down It Comes

Dick said, "I can make a house.

A big house for two boats.

A house for the yellow boat.

And for the blue boat.

See my big house."

Jane said, "I can make a house.

A big house for three cars.

Red and blue and yellow cars."

Sally said, "I can make a house.

A little house for Tim.

Here is my house for Tim.

Tim is in it.

Tim can play in it.

Oh, oh, oh.

Tim looks funny in the house."

"See my house," said Dick.
"Down it comes."

"Oh, see my house," said Jane.
"Down, down it comes."

"Oh, oh, oh," said Sally.
"Down comes my little house.
Run away, Puff.
Run away, Spot.
You can not play here."

Away We Go

Sally said, "Away we go.
Away we go in the car.
Mother and Father.
Dick and Jane.
Sally and Tim."

Dick said, "Spot is not here.
Puff is not here."

Dick said, "I see something.

Look down, Jane.

Look down and see something.

It is funny.

Can you see it?"

"Oh, oh," said Jane.

"Here is Spot."

"Come in, Spot," said Jane.
"You can go in the car."

"Away we go," said Sally.
"Away we go in the car.
Mother and Father.
Dick and Jane.
Sally and Tim and Spot.
Away we go in the big car."

Three Big Cookies

"Cookies, cookies," said Sally.
"One, two, three cookies.
Three cookies for me."

"Three big cookies," said Jane.
"Three big cookies for me."

"Cookies, cookies," said Dick.
"Three big cookies for me."

"Cookies, cookies," said Sally.
"See the three big cookies.
One for Dick and one for Jane.
One for me and one for Spot."

Dick said, "Oh, you funny baby.
Where is the one for Spot?
Where, oh, where?"

"Here, Spot," said Sally.
"Here is a cookie for you."

"Oh, oh," said Jane.
"Where is one for Sally?"

"Here it is," said Mother.
"Here is a cookie for Sally.
A big, big cookie for Sally."

See It Go

Jane said, "Look, look.
I see a big yellow car.
See the yellow car go."

Sally said, "I see it.
I see the big yellow car.
I want to go away in it.
I want to go away, away."

Dick said, "Look up, Sally.
You can see something.
It is red and yellow.
It can go up, up, up.
It can go away."

Sally said, "I want to go up.
I want to go up in it.
I want to go up, up, up.
I want to go away, away."

"Look, Sally," said Dick.
"Here is Father in a boat.
You can go away in it."

"Jump in, jump in," said Father.
"Jump in the big blue boat."

"We can go," said Sally.
"We can go away in a boat.
Away in a big blue boat."

The Blue Boat

Jane said, "See the red boat.
See the yellow boat."

Dick said, "I see the two blue boats.
Two little blue boats."

Sally said, "I see the boats.
A big yellow boat.
A little red boat.
And two blue boats.
Yellow, red, and blue."

"Oh, my," said Baby Sally.

"Tim is not here.

Where is Tim?

Oh, Jane.

Help me.

Help me find Tim."

"Look, Baby Sally," said Jane.
"See Spot jump in.
Spot can find Tim for you."

"Oh, oh," said Dick.
"See Spot go."

"Here comes Spot," said Jane.
"Here comes Spot to the boat."

"Oh, oh," said Baby Sally.
"Here comes Spot.
And here comes Tim."

BASIC READERS

THE NEW **We Look**
· and See

THE NEW

Look

Look, look.

Oh, oh, oh.

Oh, oh.

Oh, look.

Jane

Oh, Jane.

Look, Jane, look.

Look, look.

Oh, look.

See Jane.

See, see.

See Jane.

Oh, see Jane.

Dick

Look, Jane.
Look, look.
See Dick.

See, see.

Oh, see.

See Dick.

Oh, see Dick.

Oh, oh, oh.

Funny, funny Dick.

Sally

Look, Dick.
Look, Jane.
See Sally.

Oh, oh, oh.

Oh, Dick.

See Sally.

Look, Jane.

Look, Dick.

See funny Sally.

Funny, funny Sally.

Spot

Come, come.
Come, Spot, come.
Run, run, run.

Jump, Spot.

Jump, jump.

Jump, Spot, jump.

Oh, Spot.

Oh, oh, oh.

Funny, funny Spot.

Look and See

Look, Spot.

Look, Puff.

Look and see.

See Sally and Tim.

Come, Spot, come.

Jump up.

See Puff jump.

Jump up, Spot.

Jump up.

Come, Dick, come.

Come and see.

See Tim.

See Spot and Puff.

Look, Dick, look.

Oh, See

Look, Sally, look.

Look down.

Look down, Sally.

Look down, down, down.

Look up, Sally.
Look up, up, up.
Run, Sally, run.
Run and jump.
Run and jump up.

Look, Jane.

Look and see.

Oh, see.

See funny, funny Sally.